Elizabeth's Garden

Phillip Leighton-Daly

Print information available on the last page

Rev. date: 08/28/2019

To order additional copies of this book, contact:
Xlibris
1-800-455-039
www.xlibris.com.au
Orders@Xlibris.com.au

Elizabeth's Garden

Phillip Leighton-Daly
Illustrated by Windel Eborlas

The mountain grade sorely tested the two aged companions. Its steepness, the heat, and the prickly dry sclerophyll scrub all contributed toward their distress. The old man began to doubt himself. "Perhaps I've brought you up the wrong mountain," he wryly told his friend.

Any doubts that they may have harboured were quickly dispersed. There, immediately before them, loomed the mission. As stark and imposing as it may had been, there was little doubt that nature had seized control. The bush was relentlessly reclaiming its own. Trees of inordinate sizes had sprouted within the roofless maze of rooms and corridors.

The couple scaled the sandstone steps to the front balcony. Turning and facing the north, they delighted in the panoramic views of the Hawkesbury River. This was how he remembered it. Unlike humankind, it remained seemingly unaltered by the years' condemnation.

Just as an excited little boy in a candy shop, the old man immediately led his companion to the back of the building where an old garden bed was clearly defined. And there it was, a lone grave buried in the garden itself. A worn inscription on the sandstone read, "Elizabeth Davies 16 years." The old man fell to his knees and crossed himself. He remained there for several minutes, tears trailing down his cheeks. His companion lay a comforting hand on his shoulder. The grave had reopened a dreadful wound.

With an arm comforting her senior partner, the couple returned to the front balcony. With the magnificent waterway glistening in the distance, they sat on elongated slabs of sandstone. Here, where lichens decorate the pockmarked mantle stones, the old man proceeded to talk about Elizabeth.

"Liza and her parents etched out a living on the flats of the Hawkesbury River in the early 1800s. It was an uncertain existence for regular floods swept away crops, dwellings, animals, and in some cases, the settlers themselves.

"I first met Liza at the monthly church meetings on an island. Why on an island in the middle of a river you ask? The Hawkesbury River provided the earliest thoroughfare to the interior in NSW. Here on Bar Island, where two great arms of that river diverge, a church was established. After a month's isolation, the parishioners anticipated inspirational sermons, rousing choruses, sumptuous food, and convivial companionship.

"The fateful events of one particular morning are seared indelibly in my memory. Having recently arrived at the church, I keenly anticipated the arrival of other boats. Suddenly, the silence was shattered by pistol fire!

Minutes before, one mile downstream, Liza and her parents were making slow progress in a rowboat toward the church. Pirates concealed in the mangroves burst onto the river. Brandishing pistols, they surrounded the family and demanded valuables. In an attempt to protect them, Liza's father lunged forward. Sharp retorts scattered shags from the angophoras. Those contorted, voiceless sentinels hung from the cliffs in silent judgement. Mortally stricken, Mr Clarke crumpled backward into the river. His body sank beneath the swirling, muddy current. He did not resurface.

"Soon after this horrific event, Liza and her mum returned to their acreage. Devastating floods drove them closer to ruination; nightmarish thoughts of molestation by river pirates weighed heavily on their mind. Out of Christian kindness, my dad, the reverend of the mission, welcomed them to live with us. We provided comfort and care for those downtrodden by the lawless bands rampaging throughout the sparsely settled district.

"Liza settled well into life with us. She loved gardening. We enriched the sandy loam on the mountain ridge with alluvial soil from the river flats. A mountain stream provided water; a cow, fertilizer. Liza delighted in cooking her vegetables for the mission's foundlings. She grew citrus, too, several orange and lemon trees. Dad sang her praises regularly, believing that she raised the spirits of all at the mission. I felt similarly, but my shyness prevented me saying so.

"The indigenous people of the district befriended us. From them we learnt much about bush tucker. We flavoured our drinks with the nectar from banksia, paperbark, and grass tree flowers. The Aboriginal people led us to secluded pockets of towering Port Jackson fig trees. We ate the raw fruit. Paddies were a favourite for breakfast. We mashed the figs up, mixed them with flour, and fried them in a skillet. The Aboriginal people shaped an oven for us from a termites' nest. They cut a chimney in the top and a side aperture into which we could cook all kinds of food.

"The mission afforded some protection for the victims of the lawless. I say some protection for, at best, we provided temporary respite. My dad deplored the lawlessness endemic along the river. As Christian-minded as he may have been, he was often heard to say, 'Hell is empty; the devils are here.'¹

---

1. William Shakespeare, The Tempest Translation (online), Act 1, Scene 2, p.10.

9

"After the murder of Liza's father, our families harboured smouldering resentment for the river pirates. Heated exchanges frequently occurred between Liza and Sergeant Smythe, the local policeman. Liza's outbursts were fuelled from both her father's death and the police's indifference toward it. 'The pirates are inhuman devils,' she complained to the sergeant.

"'The pirates are escaped convicts operating on the river,' said the sergeant assuredly. He took great satisfaction in correcting Liza. 'They will be caught and brought to justice.'

"But intellectually, Liza was more than a match for the sergeant. 'Aboriginal warriors contribute more toward the recapture of these felons than you, Sergeant,' she mocked him. 'I have heard that in the north, the warriors spear them in retribution for indecent assaults on their own people. Sometimes they surround them and strip them of their clothes at spear point. They march them off to the authorities.[2] How do you reward them, Sergeant?' And after a brief pause, she continued, 'You give them pieces of threadbare blankets, corn, or rations of bad spirits for their trouble.[3] The runaways are more fearful of the Aboriginal trackers than they are of you!'

2 J. W. Turner. *Newcastle as a Convict Settlement: The Evidence before J. T. Bigge in 1819 – 1821*. Newcastle Public Library, Newcastle, 1973, p. 85.
3 Ibid., p. 86.

"'The blacks should tend to their own business,' said the sergeant with a malicious sneer.

"'Nor should the pirates murder settlers on the river,' replied Liza in an equally sardonic tone. 'The pirates are in league with Satan. Come inside the mission, and note the suffering that they have brought upon the residents there.'

"The sergeant was well beaten, and he knew it. He dared not step into the mission for he knew what lay there. 'Take care, miss.' He sneered hatefully, pointing his finger accusingly at Liza. 'The reverend cannot protect you for sedition.'

"To that, Liza rolled her eyes, threw her hands in to the air, and stormed away. 'You must watch that one,' the sergeant snapped at my father.

"We all viewed the sergeant as a buffoon and took little notice of his officious ramblings. Many police of this era were ex-convicts, and corrupt, drunken layabouts. And soon after he had ridden off over the ridge, my dad offered Liza precious words of encouragement: 'Idle words are like weeds. They require no sowing!'

"Liza drew much inspiration from this advice and mentioned it to me several times after. 'I won't tolerate weeds in my garden,' she said.

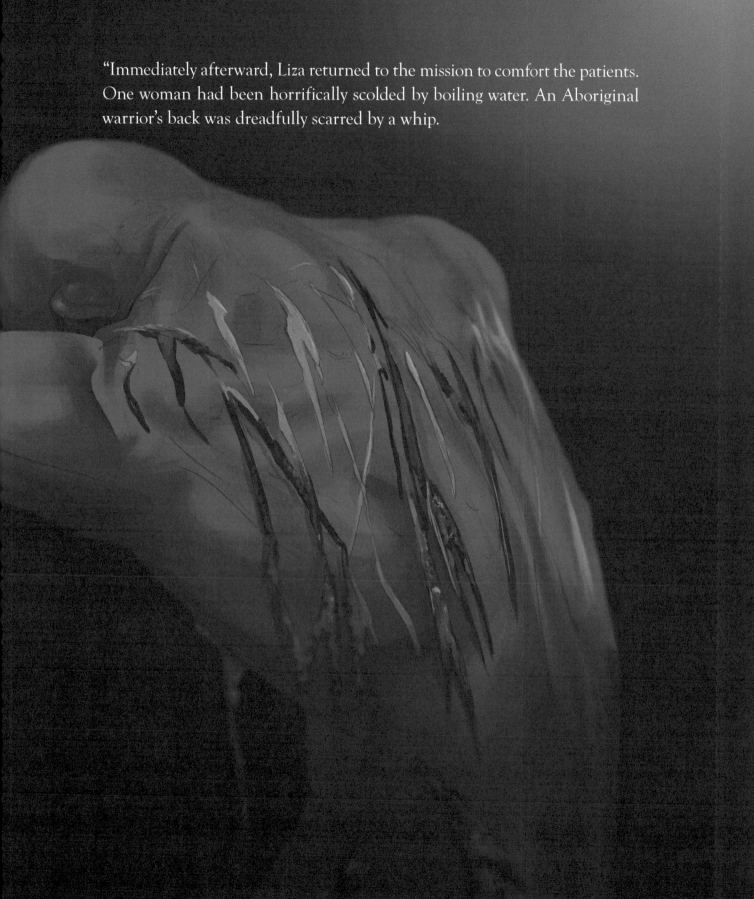

"Immediately afterward, Liza returned to the mission to comfort the patients. One woman had been horrifically scolded by boiling water. An Aboriginal warrior's back was dreadfully scarred by a whip.

A young settler spent his wakeful hours motionless, gazing out the window. Not that he could see anything, for his eyes had been scoured out with sticks. His skilful athleticism, his glorious hunting exploits had been criminally stolen. A congealed bloody eye bandage was a stark instance of human brutality.

"Dad's opinion of the justice system was far more severe than ours. He held secretive liaisons with numerous sympathizers, namely indigenous freedom fighters such as Pemulwuy and his son Tedbury, and others such as the Wesley Church, and select bushrangers. They all served as informants in addressing the lawlessness.

"My father's liaisons with Aboriginal freedom fighters involved a terrible risk. These fearless warriors struck out decisively against the extermination policy employed by the European settlers. And even though the governor placed massive bounties on Pemulwuy's head, my father strongly believed that Aboriginal reprisals were largely due to the injustice initially handed out to them.

"Pemulwuy's death had a devastating effect on my Dad. His body was horribly mutilated; his head was placed in a bottle of spirits and dispatched to Joseph Banks in England.

"While alive, Pemulwuy was vilified by Governor King. Trumped-up charges and hefty bounties quickly led to his murder. The bounties included conditional emancipations, pardons, and twenty gallons of liquor.

"The barbaric mutilation of Permulwuy's body resulted in public outcries. A hurried reassessment by Governor King ensued. Pemulwuy, he declared, was a brave and independent warrior, a man who inspired others and died for his land and people. For those reasons, the governor announced that he should be admired and respected.[4]

"That Dad collaborated with bushrangers may shock you. Some convict bushrangers, such as the Swing Rioters in England, were sentenced for social injustice. In this instance, they were transported for protesting about the thousands of peasants perishing from starvation.

"Many large landholders, magistrates, and police, on the other hand, were horribly corrupt in colonial days. In some Newcastle and Wollongong districts, they were seen as the criminals.[5] The police force did not earn respectability until 1870.[6]

"If you find it difficult to visualize church parishioners involved in fighting lawlessness, you should consider the North American example. The Abolitionists played a greater role in freeing slaves than President Abraham Lincoln.

---

4 National Museum of Australia, Pemulway (internet); J. L. Kohen, "Pemulway 1750 – 1802, *Australian Dictionary of Biology*.
5 John Vader, Red Gold: The Tree that Built the Nation. Sydney, 2002, p. 63.
6 Admissions readily apparent in the Police and Justice Museum, Circular Quay, Sydney.

"Toward the antics of one group of escaped convicts, my father held absolute condemnation. His opinion of the cedar cutters reflected those in the newspapers. 'Consisting of run-a-ways and other bad characters who flock to these places, they are almost beyond the pale of the law committing scenes of vice and infamy, we are informed, too horrible to contemplate.'[7]

"On a ridge above a secluded grassy knoll, Liza and I witnessed the cedar gang's debauchery. Sustained by gallons of grog supplied by illicit dealers, revellers drank themselves into oblivion. Abducted women and children were abused, gambling was rife, and drunken fights were frequent. Many of the participants harvested timber and burnt shells for lime and mangroves for ash. Soda ash (mangroves) was used in the production of soap.

_____

7 John Vader, *Red Gold: The Tree that Built the Nation*, Sydney, 2002 p.60.

"This loud and undisciplined group on the grassy knoll not only involved runaways. Merchants, squatters and others revelled in ghoulish, unprincipled depravity. [8]

"Though many of the participants were unknown to us, several were quickly recognized. 'There's Sergeant Smythe,' gasped Liza. 'And look there; his constables too.'

8 Ibid., p. 60.

"Near where this revelry took place, the river pirates concealed stolen vessels in the mangrove swamps. From the river, no entranceway was discernible. On brushing the mangroves aside, a distinct passage emerged through them. A channel had been excavated and led to a widened enclosure. Stolen rowboats lay on their sides in the mud. Access was negotiable only at full tide; the channel was otherwise too shallow for deep hulled vessels. Viewed from the river, no hint of the stolen boatyard could be seen.

"It became our intention to steal a boat during the drunken revelry. At dusk, as the flow of the incoming tide approached its peak, Liza and I heaved a clinker rowboat through black oozing mud into the main arm of the river. Climbing aboard, we rowed directly to the eastern bank. A frenetic current swept us upstream.

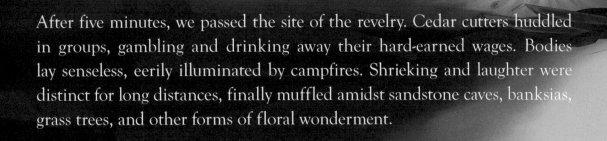

After five minutes, we passed the site of the revelry. Cedar cutters huddled in groups, gambling and drinking away their hard-earned wages. Bodies lay senseless, eerily illuminated by campfires. Shrieking and laughter were distinct for long distances, finally muffled amidst sandstone caves, banksias, grass trees, and other forms of floral wonderment.

"Occasional strokes of our oars were needed to keep our bow pointed upstream. With these we took particular care for the clash of an oar on a gunwale echoed distinctly. We remained deathly silent, too, as sound travels long distances over a large body of water.

"At a point near the mission, Calabash Creek trailed through a maze of mangroves. We overturned the boat in this quiet backwater, covering it with branches.[9] Then we climbed up several hundred yards to the mission directly above. Several days after, it was no surprise when Sergeant Smythe paid us a visit. He inquired about the thieving of settlers' boats!

"In our sojourns around the bush, Liza and I encountered many distressing scenes of the cedar cutters' handiwork. We recovered two distraught children crying beside the bodies of their dead parents. We took these orphans back to the mission, where we afforded them emergency care. As with the Abolitionists in the USA, my dad ran an underground railway. Young children were taken firstly by boat to Windsor and thence to the estates of landholders such as John and William Macarthur. These and other sympathisers organized adoptions for the orphaned children.

"Strewn about the bush were remnants of the cedar cutters' handiwork. Mutilated bodies of wombats, echidnas, koalas, and kangaroos rotted in the bushland. We recovered live babies from their dead mothers' pouches. Numerous snakes and lizards were strung over tree branches, and platypus carcasses were occasionally encountered by the river. There appeared no limit to the cedar cutters' wastefulness.

---

9 The sandstone ruin high up on the ridge above Calabash Creek gave me the idea for the story. It was established as a guest house around 1900 and was known as Fretus's Inn. Further information on the internet under the search 'Ruined Castle of Calabash' can be found.

"Having learnt where these animals imprisoned their victims, Liza and I boldly conceived a plan to rescue them. With the ringing of axes resounding in the distance, we were reassured that the cedar cutters were slaughtering away in the bush. I say slaughtering, for like a sickle, these sawyers illegally pilfered the forestry stands while reaping havoc among all life along the Hawkesbury. 'Shoot it if it moves' was a popular catchcry, 'or if it doesn't, cut it down.'[10]

"On entering one crude stringybark hut, Liza and I were confronted by a disturbing scene. Two females and three children lay tightly bound and gagged on the floor. Without incident, we led them safely to the mission.

"Two weeks after this rescue, Liza and I launched our stolen vessel into the main arm of the river. Aboard were the three orphaned children. Ours was the simple task of rowing them to Marramarra Creek, a short distance away. Sarah Ferdinand, an Aboriginal lady, lived there with her German husband, a former convict. They had seven children.

"The ebb current pushed us along at breakneck speed. Half a mile from the rendezvous, we became greatly distressed as several hundred yards behind, pirates were rapidly closing on us. With four oarsmen powering each boat, Liza and I feared we would soon be overtaken.

---

10 An anonymous Australian outcry.

"Just as all hope seemed lost, the pirates, in an attempt to reduce the distance even more, steered close to the western shore. With the tide rushing furiously out to sea, they found themselves high and dry on a muddy shoal. To continue, they had to disembark and manhandle their boat through black, oozing sludge into deeper water.

"But we now had to change our plans. We could no longer rendezvous at Marramarra Creek. It was now within the pirates' view. To do so would surely result in savage reprisals for the Ferdinand family.

"Further downstream, out of view of the pirates, we disembarked and pushed our unmanned boat out into the sweeping current. We escorted the orphans upstream to the Ferdinands' homestead.

"On returning along the foreshore, we noted that the pirates had gone. Plainly they had manhandled their boats into the river. Half an hour later, we noticed them again; they had recovered our stolen boat! As we huddled on the western shoreline, with their boats passing midstream, Liza's world suddenly fell apart. 'I've left my cardigan in the boat. It must have fallen beneath the seat in our panic.'

"When we reported the incident to Dad, he told us not to worry and that he would settle it. He planned to send Liza to live with the Macarthurs. On the day before this event, the sergeant called, accompanied by several constables. My dad greeted him cordially, but the sergeant was in no mood for pleasantries. 'Elizabeth has much to answer for. Her cardigan was found in a stolen rowboat.'

"'How do you know it was Elizabeth's?'

"'It has her name in it!' There wasn't much else we could say. Still, Dad refused to cooperate. The police drew their cutlasses, and the situation threatened to turn ugly.

"'I insist upon accompanying her,' my dad said.

"I moved close to Liza. Placing a consoling arm around her shoulder, I said, 'I'm going too.'

"'If that's what you want,' said the sergeant, grinning quizzically at the two constables.

"'I shall need to gather belongings,'" said Dad.

"'You have five minutes,' snapped the sergeant.

"'So my crimes are adjudged more serious than those who murdered my father?' cried the distraught teenager. The sergeant did not answer. There was nothing in truth that he could possibly say.

"My dad entered the rear rooms of the mission. He had anticipated trouble such as this. Standing by a wall were three bushrangers: Mick Malone, Ned Taylor, and John Boatman. Each was heavily armed. 'Follow us from a distance,' Dad instructed. John and Ned nodded. Mad Mick grinned, shook his head curiously, and rolled his eyes. He was known as Mad Mick for his manner of shaking his head. People likened it to someone rattling their brains.

"We reassured Liza's mother that we would not return without her daughter safe in hand.

"As we wound down the track to the river, several armed ruffians closed in from behind. I warned Dad, who appeared unperturbed, that all was well in hand.

"Under the pretence that he had stepped upon a snake, the sergeant halted. 'I'm sorry that it has come to this,' he said. 'You simply know too much. We'll blame your deaths on the Aboriginal people.'

"Suddenly, the two rogues fell, struck by flying objects. Liza grabbed my arm protectively, shielding my body from danger and leading me towards a grove of grasstrees. But the constable's pistol ball struck Liza squarely in the back. Without a sound, her limp body crashed down upon me. My dad ran quickly to her aid. As the constable raised his gun to shoot him, both the constable and the sergeant fell to a volley of pistol fire. A lone constable fled into the scrub.

"Blood-curdling screams indicated that he met a terrifying end. No amount of searching ever recovered the body of that constable. To this day, we do not know who killed the two rogues. Both died from severe head traumas.

"We carried Liza's body back to the mission, back to her inconsolable mother. We buried her in her beloved vegetable garden.

"Though the disappearance of the officers caused an almighty hue and cry, there was an absence of any real evidence. It was decided to blame it on the Aboriginal people.

"Following the death of her daughter, Mrs Clarke moved to Parramatta, where she worked at the Wesley Mission. She married a church official and adopted one of the three children that Liza and I rescued. She named her Beth, after her daughter. 'There will never be another, Elizabeth,' she told me."

Having related the sad plight of Liza, the old man shook his head and sighed with resignation. His companion assisted him to his feet, and they moved once again to the garden. The pair noted the most beautiful flowers growing there. "Liza's raising wildflowers these days," he said.

"Do you realize," remarked the lady, "I have no recollection of any of those events."

"Don't trouble yourself with that, Beth," the old man added.

And as the two companions stood gazing upon the garden bed, assorted memories flooded back to them. There alluvial river mud was carried sixty years ago; there Liza grew her vegetables, and there beneath that profusion of native flowers, she rests peacefully today.

Then as if recalling a distant memory, the old man knelt down and plucked weeds from around the headstone. His aged companion stared quizzically at him. "Liza never tolerated weeds, " the old man told her.

He rose shakily to his feet, and gazed longingly at the grave as if for the last time. Then with her arms around the others waist, the two companions made their way down to the river.

An adaption of John Greenleaf Whittier's poem "School Days,"

1807 –1899. (Public Domain)

Still memory to a grey-haired man,
That sweet child face is showing.
Dear girl! The grasses on her grave
Have fifty years been growing!

He lives to learn in life's hard school
How few who pass around him
Lament his triumph and her loss
Like him because she loved him.

CPSIA information can be obtained
at www.ICGtesting.com
Printed in the USA
BVHW021931080919
557875BV00003B/39/P